LITTLE MISS TROUBLE
moving house

Original concept by Roger Hargreaves
Illustrated and written by Adam Hargreaves

Little Miss Trouble lives in Uptonogood Cottage surrounded by fields and trees and more fields and more trees, and even more fields.

Her nearest neighbours live miles and miles away and there is a very good reason for this.

That very good reason is Miss Trouble!

Nobody wants to live next door to somebody who causes so much trouble.

Somebody who telephoned Mr Lazy at
5 o'clock every morning for a whole week.

And somebody who told Mr Wrong that the best thing to use to polish his car was boot polish.

Now, because she lived all on her own, Miss Trouble found that she could not cause half as much trouble as she would like to.

What Little Miss Trouble longed for more than anything else was a neighbour.

One Monday when Little Miss Trouble was walking in the woods near her house she came upon a wishing well.

"Well, I never," she said, and then she had an idea. She threw a coin in the well.

"I wish I lived next door to ... somebody," she said out loud.

Later that day when she looked out of her window, she discovered that, as if by magic, which it was, her house was next door to Box Cottage, which is where Mr Chatterbox lives.

"Tee hee, now for some fun!" giggled Miss Trouble.

She crept down the lane, around the corner, up a telegraph pole and cut the telephone line!

Poor Mr Chatterbox.

No telephone.

No one to chat to.

But it was then that he looked out the window and saw Miss Trouble's house.

Five minutes later there was a knock at Little Miss Trouble's door.

"Hello," said Mr Chatterbox. "Just thought I'd pop round for a quick chat. Funny thing, you know, my telephone's broken and ... "

And Mr Chatterbox talked and chatted and chatted and talked through the morning, all afternoon and late into the night.

The next day, Tuesday, a very tired Little Miss Trouble went back to the wishing well and threw in another coin. "I wish that I lived next door to someone else," she said.

And the very next morning Little Miss Trouble found herself living next door to Mr Bump.

She threw tiny stones at his window to wake him up. And smashed the window!

But Mr Bump has so many accidents that he did not notice one more broken window.

Little Miss Trouble went back to the wishing well.

On Wednesday Miss Trouble tried to play a trick on Little Miss Lucky. But she discovered that Miss Lucky is too lucky for any of Miss Trouble's tricks to work on her.

On Thursday there was nobody in at Little Miss Late's house.

She was late getting back from her holiday!

On Friday Little Miss Trouble told Mr Muddle that Mr Small had called him an egg-head.

But Mr Muddle got muddled up and instead of being angry with Mr Small he thanked him!

On Saturday Little Miss Trouble let the tyres down on Mr Forgetful's car.

But Mr Forgetful forgot he had a car and caught the bus.

On Sunday it was a very fed up Little Miss Trouble who returned to the wishing well to make a wish.

And then she had a thought.

A thought that went like this, "The trouble with neighbours," thought Little Miss Trouble, "is that they are too much trouble!"

And she went home and was very, very good and didn't make any trouble for anybody for ever and ever ...

... well, until Tuesday!

3 Great Offers For Mr Men Fans

1 Token EGMONT WORLD

1 FREE Door Hangers and Posters

In every Mr Men and Little Miss Book like this one you will find a special token. Collect 6 and we will send you either a brilliant Mr. Men or Little Miss poster and a Mr Men or Little Miss double sided, full colour, bedroom door hanger. Apply using the coupon overleaf, enclosing six tokens and a 50p coin for your choice of two items.

Egmont World tokens can be used towards any other Egmont World / World International token scheme promotions, in early learning and story / activity books.

Posters: Tick your preferred choice of either Mr Men ☐ or Little Miss ☐

Door Hangers: Choose from: Mr. Nosey & Mr Muddle ☐, Mr Greedy & Mr Lazy ☐, Mr Tickle & Mr Grumpy ☐, Mr Slow & Mr Busy ☐, Mr Messy & Mr Quiet ☐, Mr Perfect & Mr Forgetful ☐, Little Miss Fun & Little Miss Late ☐, Little Miss Helpful & Little Miss Tidy ☐, Little Miss Busy & Little Miss Brainy ☐, Little Miss Star & Little Miss Fun ☐.
(Please tick)

ENTRANCE FEE 3 SAUSAGES

2 Mr Men Library Boxes

Keep your growing collection of Mr Men and Little Miss books in these superb library boxes. With an integral carrying handle and stay-closed fastener, these full colour, plastic boxes are fantastic. They are just £5.49 each including postage. Order overleaf.

3 Join The Club

To join the fantastic Mr Men & Little Miss Club, check out the page overleaf NOW!

· RETURN THIS WHOLE PAGE ·

Join Our Club!

When you become a member of the fantastic Mr Men and Little Miss Club you'll receive a personal letter from Mr Happy and Little Miss Giggles, a club badge with your name, and a superb Welcome Pack (pictured below right).

You'll also get birthday and Christmas cards from the Mr Men and Little Misses, 2 newsletters crammed with special offers, privileges and news, and a copy of the 12 page Mr Men catalogue which includes great party ideas.

If it were on sale in the shops, the Welcome Pack alone might cost around £13. But a year's membership is just £9.99 (plus 73p postage) with a 14 day money-back guarantee if you are not delighted!

HOW TO APPLY To apply for any of these three great offers, ask an adult to complete the coupon below and send it with appropriate payment and tokens (where required) to: Mr Men Offers, PO Box 7, Manchester M19 2HD. Credit card orders for Club membership ONLY by telephone, please call: 01403 242727.

To be completed by an adult

❏ **1.** Please send a poster and door hanger as selected overleaf. I enclose six tokens and a 50p coin for post (coin not required if you are also taking up 2. or 3. below).

❏ **2.** Please send __ Mr Men Library case(s) and __ Little Miss Library case(s) at £5.49 each.

❏ **3.** Please enrol the following in the Mr Men & Little Miss Club at £10.72 (inc postage)

Fan's Name:_____Fan's Address:_____

_____Post Code:_____Date of birth:___/___/___

Your Name:_____Your Address:_____

Post Code:_____Name of parent or guardian (if not you):_____

Total amount due: £_____ (£5.49 per Library Case, £10.72 per Club membership)

❏ I enclose a cheque or postal order payable to Egmont World Limited.

❏ Please charge my MasterCard / Visa account.

Card number: | | | | | | | | | | | | | | | | |

Expiry Date: _____/_____   Signature: _____

Data Protection Act: If you do **not** wish to receive other family offers from us or companies we recommend, please tick this box ❏. Offer applies to UK only